Bird

Cat

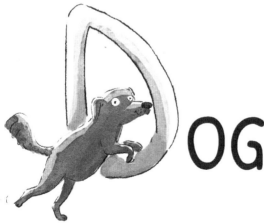

Dog

written by Jenny Watt
illustrated by Begüm Manav

Bird Cat Dog

Written by Jenny Watt

Illustrated by Begüm Manav

ISBN 979-8-533640-84-8

For Leela

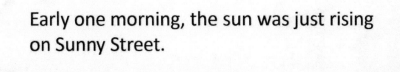

Early one morning, the sun was just rising on Sunny Street.

Dog shook his fur and got ready to chase Cat.

Cat stretched her legs and got ready to chase Bird.

But Bird, sitting high up in the tree, felt
a little different that morning.

He thought, "Why do I run away from Cat every day? I run so that she can have fun. But what do I get? Not even a Thank You."

Cat, who was sitting at the bottom of the tree, was getting impatient.

"Hey Birdie, are you ready to shake your feathers and fly away so I can chase you?" she asked cheerfully.

"I'm ready Cat, but I'm not flying today."

"Not flying today?" said Cat, surprised. "But then I'll catch you."

"I know, but why should I fly around every day just so that you and Dog can have your fun? Neither of you have said Thank You, not even once," said Bird.

Cat thought for a minute and tried another tact.

"Look here Bird, it is only natural for us to run after you.

You are B for Bird. I'm C for Cat. And Dog is D for Dog.

Now you know that the alphabet goes B, C and then D."

"Then why don't you go and chase a ball, or a bumblebee then? They start with B too."

Cat was in trouble. Bird was smarter than she thought.

She went to see Dog. "Can we start now?" asked Dog.

Cat shook her head. "Sorry Dog, but Bird won't fly."

"What do you mean, Bird won't fly?" asked Dog.

"Bird said he's tired of running away every day. And he's upset that we never said Thank You to him."

"But he has to run, Cat!" said Dog. "He's a bird! You're a cat! And I'm a dog. It's only natural!"

They thought for a moment.

Then Cat said, "It's simple. Bird doesn't know how much we like him."

"Then why don't we do something to show him that we care," said Dog.

Cat said, "Okay, but what can we do?"

"What about his birthday? Why don't we celebrate his birthday?"

"Good idea," said Cat. "Oh Bird!" she called up to Bird.

Bird flew down to a lower branch.

"Bird, when is your birthday?"

Bird shook his head. "I don't know. I never had one."

Cat and Dog looked at each other. Never had a birthday! No wonder he was unhappy.

Dog had an idea.

He said, "Listen here, Bird. You probably don't know it, but today just happens to be a special day for all birds. Today is Happy Bird Day."

"Happy Bird Day! What's that?" asked Bird.

"It's the one day in the year when the whole world says Thank you to all you birds for being so pretty," said Cat.

"And cheerful," added Dog.

"And musical," said Cat.

"And, just to show you how much we love you,
Bird, we're going to sing you a special song."

Happy Bird Day to YOU!
Happy Bird Day to YOU!
Happy BIRD DAY dear BIRDIE,
Happy Bird Day to YOU!

Bird was so happy he almost fell off the tree branch.

"Why, thank you Cat and Dog," Bird said shyly. "I didn't know you sang so well."

Dog and Cat were also pleased with themselves.

Cat looked at Dog and said, "You know Dog, I'm a little tired of the same routine, day after day. Why don't we have a picnic instead."

"That's a great idea," said Dog. "Hey Bird, do you want to have a picnic with us?"

Bird said, "As long as you promise not to chase me."

Both Cat and Dog put up their paws. "We promise."

So the three friends sat in the garden and talked, instead of running around like animals.

And the next day, Bird let Cat chase him again, and Dog chased Cat, and Bird didn't mind at all.

Because the day after that, Bird chased Cat, and Cat chased Dog, and Dog had to run away!

Printed in Great Britain
by Amazon